THIS UNICORN BOOK BELONGS TO

....

Can A Unicorn Help Me Deal With Bullying?
My Unicorn Books - Volume 4
Written by Steve Herman

ISBN: 978-1-950280-16-2 (paperback)
ISBN: 978-1-950280-17-9 (hardcover)

www.MyUnicornBooks.com

First Edition: October 2019
10 9 8 7 6 5 4 3 2 1

I'm Allie, and I'm back again – Do you remember me?
I'm the girl who has a unicorn that I call Dazzle D.

The "D" stand for "Delight," and if you knew her, you'd admit
That Dazzle is delightful, and her name's a perfect fit.

Dazzle taught me to be confident and hold my head up high,
And to make my choices wisely and not be scared to try.

She taught me something recently – I can hardly wait to tell!
This lesson Dazzle taught me, might help others out, as well!

Dazzle noticed I was sad, and, of course, she wondered why,
So I told her what had happened as I tried hard not to cry.

I said, "A girl named Marcy has decided I'm The One -
She's chosen me to pick on - That's why school's no longer fun."

And though I tried to hold it back,
a tear rolled down my cheek
As I told my Dazzle D
all about my dreadful week.

Dazzle is my dearest friend, so I shared with her about...
The awful things I had endured - It all came pouring out.

It started in the lunchroom when I found a place to sit,
And Marcy and her friends all came and threw a major fit.

"You can't sit here!" she told me as they all began to fuss –
"Everybody knows," she said, "this table's just for us!"

All day long I noticed that those girls all were staring,
And making fun of me and the clothes that I was wearing.

They said bad things about me. They called me names.
They said mean things that really put me to shame.

Soon others would not play with me, for all of them knew,
She'd pick on them, as well, for that's what Marcy liked to do.

I told Dazzle all about how that made me feel blue,
Then I asked Dazzle if she thought
what Marcy said was *true!*

Dazzle tried to comfort me.
She said, "Allie, I prefer...
To think the problem's not with you,
but rather, it's with her".

"Some people are not loved enough
and have no love to give,
And they've not figured out quite yet,
that that's no way to live."

"Or maybe no one's taught them and they simply have no clue
That all the love you give away will come right back to you."

"I see that Marcy has some friends
who let her take the lead –
But you can trust me, Allie Girl,
those aren't the friends you need!"

"Those kids might be afraid
that they'll be bullied, too;
That's why they choose to be with her
and not be nice to you."

"A bully's words can really hurt –
I admit that this is true,
But when you're being bullied,
there are things you must not do.
Don't be just like the bully
and say mean things in return –
No fight ever ends that way –
This is something you must learn."

Soon I had the chance to take my unicorn's advice
When Marcy made a comment and it wasn't very nice.

Then one day I invited all the kids to fly up to the sky,
For Dazzle D was giving rides and taking us up high...
Above the clouds where rainbows were
and letting us slide down –
It was like a playground in the clouds,
way up above the town!

Then Marcy asked, "May I go, too?"
My friends told her, "No!
You've been mean to Allie;
that's why we won't let you go."

But I recalled what Dazzle said
and decided to be **kind** –
"Come along!" I said to Marcy,
"Don't get left behind!"

Now Marcy's learning bit by bit, each and every day
That if you want to have *true* friends, **kindness** is the way.

READ MORE ABOUT ALLIE AND DAZZLE!

VISIT WWW.MYUNICORNBOOKS.COM

Lightning Source UK Ltd.
Milton Keynes UK
UKHW050721220721
387412UK00007B/150